EGMONT

We bring stories to life

First published in Great Britain in 2007 by Dean,
an imprint of Egmont UK Limited
239 Kensington High Street, London W8 6SA

Thomas the Tank Engine & Friends™

A BRITT ALLCROFT COMPANY PRODUCTION

Based on The Railway Series by The Reverend W Awdry
Photographs © 2007 Gullane (Thomas) LLC. A HIT Entertainment Company

Thomas the Tank Engine & Friends and Thomas & Friends are trademarks of Gullane (Thomas) Limited.
Thomas the Tank Engine & Friends and Design is Reg. US. Pat. & Tm. Off.

ISBN 978 0 6035 6251 8
ISBN 0 6035 6251 5
1 3 5 7 9 10 8 6 4 2
Printed in Singapore

Thomas and the Jet Engine

The Thomas TV Series

Gordon loved nothing more than speeding along the line as fast as he could, with the wind blowing across his funnel.

"I'm the fastest engine on Sodor," he boasted.

But not all the engines were impressed.

"Speed isn't everything," said James, smugly.

"But being reliable and useful is," said Thomas.

One morning, The Fat Controller arrived with news of an important job for Thomas. "I want you to collect a jet engine from the airfield," he said.

"What's a jet engine?" asked Percy.

The Fat Controller explained that a jet engine pushes hot air out of its back and goes very, very fast. As fast as a rocket.

Thomas liked making special deliveries for The Fat Controller. But secretly he wished he could go as fast as Gordon.

When Thomas arrived at the Docks, he was excited to see the jet engine. It was shiny and modern and Thomas had never seen anything like it.

Cranky was taking his time lifting the jet engine.

"Hurry up," huffed Thomas.

Cranky did not like being told what to do.

He was careless with his hook and it knocked the switch on the jet engine. The switch started the engine, and the engine began to whine.

"Uh-oh," said Cranky, and before he could say anything else, the jet engine rocketed up the track, pushing Thomas in front of it!

"Ooooooohhhhhhh!" cried Thomas. He was going faster than he had ever been before.

And faster than Gordon had ever been before!

The fields and trees were just a blur as he whizzed along the track. James and Percy watched in amazement as he flew past. No one had ever seen a tank engine go so fast!

His Driver tried to put on the brakes.

"Slow down!" he cried. "You must try to stop!"
But Thomas *couldn't* stop.

He just went faster . . . and faster. He had never been
so excited!

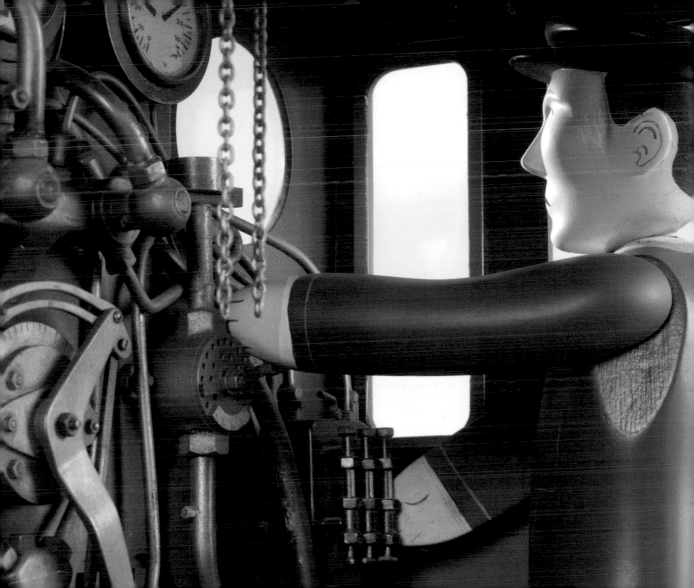

Bertie was waiting at the level crossing. He was surprised to see his friend moving so quickly.

"Want to race, Thomas?" called Bertie, as he saw Thomas approaching . . .

"Never mind," he said, as Thomas flew by.

Thomas' Driver called to the signalman to change the signals.

"Clear the lines!" he said. "It's a runaway train!" The signalman rushed to switch the points, but he was too late. Just as he reached them, he saw Thomas whooooosh by.

When Henry saw Thomas, his jaw dropped in astonishment.

"Just wait till Gordon sees you!" he called.

Thomas whizzed through a station and all the passengers on the platform stared. Thomas was such a blur that they couldn't see who he was.

"Who was that? Surely even Gordon can't go that fast!" they said to each other.

Gordon had no idea that Thomas was racing down the main line.

"I am the fastest," Gordon said to himself proudly, as he wheeshed along.

The next moment, his face fell as he saw Thomas whizzing towards him on the other track.

"Hi, Gordon . . . bye, Gordon!" whistled Thomas, as he shot past.

At last the jet engine ran out of fuel. Thomas steamed gently into Knapford Station.

"Sorry for overtaking you back there, Gordon!" teased Thomas.

"Overtaking me? I hadn't noticed," huffed Gordon.

"Didn't notice the fastest engine on Sodor?" said Henry.

"Yes, I am the fastest!" chuckled Thomas.

Percy felt a little sorry for Gordon.

"Gordon can't go as fast as a jet engine. He's only a steam engine," he said.

"But he is full of hot air!" teased James.

Gordon pretended he wasn't listening.